TURN ON THE LIGHT

Sangini Agarwal

Chennai • Bangalore

CLEVER FOX PUBLISHING
Chennai, India

Published by CLEVER FOX PUBLISHING 2023
Copyright © Sangini Agarwal 2023

All Rights Reserved.
ISBN: 978-93-56484-41-2

This book has been published with all reasonable efforts taken to make the material error-free after the consent of the author. No part of this book shall be used, reproduced in any manner whatsoever without written permission from the author, except in the case of brief quotations embodied in critical articles and reviews.

The Author of this book is solely responsible and liable for its content including but not limited to the views, representations, descriptions, statements, information, opinions and references ["Content"]. The Content of this book shall not constitute or be construed or deemed to reflect the opinion or expression of the Publisher or Editor. Neither the Publisher nor Editor endorse or approve the Content of this book or guarantee the reliability, accuracy or completeness of the Content published herein and do not make any representations or warranties of any kind, express or implied, including but not limited to the implied warranties of merchantability, fitness for a particular purpose. The Publisher and Editor shall not be liable whatsoever for any errors, omissions, whether such errors or omissions result from negligence, accident, or any other cause or claims for loss or damages of any kind, including without limitation, indirect or consequential loss or damage arising out of use, inability to use, or about the reliability, accuracy or sufficiency of the information contained in this book.

CONTENTS

Preface iv

1. #Caffeinespeakeasy 1
2. A Second Chance 8
3. Binding Shackles 16
4. Fate? Maybe Destiny? 22
5. Elevators: Awkward, Am I Right? 30
6. Puppets in a Cage 35
7. I Have a Heart to Heart With My Great-Great-Great-Grandmother 41
8. The Book of History 48
9. Death of the Sun 56

About the Author 63

PREFACE

"You should write a book."

A single light-bulb moment two years ago is what led me to begin this journey, after my dad read an essay I'd written for school.

The idea seemed absurd at the time, but, the more I thought about it, the brighter the light glowed. Even as the conscious part of my brain was rejecting the idea, my subconscious had started planning out possibilities, shaping the message I wanted to convey.

In the summer of 2020, during the massive lockdown at the peak of the hysteria that permeated the globe due to COVID-19, I commenced, albeit hesitantly. As an individual who is extremely indecisive, writing a whole book had never appealed to me as deciding on a particular set of characters was next to impossible. So, with unwavering certainty, I decided I would write a collection of short stories.

By the end of the summer, I'd written twenty five stories that were possible contenders for the final book. Year 10 began, and with that came a whole new environment with added stress of GCSEs. Caught up in the sudden shift, the book took a backseat in my mind and instead I turned to studying, making sure I got the grades I needed.

Eventually, after my maths GCSE was concluded in June, I could finally focus on the book again. Of course, since I'd written these almost a year prior, my writing had improved and the stories were not to the best of my ability. So, I set about tweaking and expanding them. Looking back with a fresh set of eyes once the veil of GCSE stress was lifted, I set out to perfect and expand the stories.

When they had been completed to my satisfaction, I turned to my mom for peer editing, who said that there should be a theme linking them all together. As soon as she'd uttered those words, I knew my theme would be renewed hope, bringing light into the darkness, inspired by the real-life events that were happening around us. It was my way of contributing something to the community, through the means of my beloved pastime.

The final product, nine short flash fiction stories, is what you see here, culminated through two years of hard work. I'm immensely proud that my dream has come to fruition, and I'm so grateful for all the people who have helped me along this journey, most of all my parents, who have been my steadfast supporters.

Although this is a bit later than planned, it is finally going to be unveiled and I could not be more excited. As the COVID era ends and a new dawn graces the horizon, I wanted to publish this as a reminder to prevail through tough times. As Dumbledore once said, "Happiness can be found even in the darkest of times, if one only remembers to turn on the light."

#Caffeinespeakeasy

What Tyler had not expected to see when he walked into the kitchen this morning was his family standing around the table in various positions of immobilisation. Dad was staring unseeingly at the television, as Mom sluggishly turned the pages of her portfolio, with an apple halfway to her mouth.

When asked what was wrong, they didn't even notice Tyler's presence, let alone actually reply. He waved his hands in front of their faces before they stirred.

"Oh, thank god," Tyler exclaimed in relief. "I thought you'd been possessed by demons or something."

"We haven't. But the government clearly has," his dad replied.

"Why? What's wrong?" Usually, Mr. Bailey was supportive of the government, so to hear him say that was dumbfounding.

"They've decided to outlaw coffee. With no warning, just on a random day." "What? No. They wouldn't do that." Mr. Bailey handed Tyler the newspaper.

The headlines read in glaring red: "*President chokes on unground coffee bean. Effective immediately, coffee is banned in the United States of America.*"

"But I don't understand why. Why haven't they banned alcohol then?"

"I don't know, but they're clearly off their rockers."

The news still hadn't sunk in. "So, no more coffee?" Tyler asked once again, flabbergasted.

"I guess so."

"But they can't do that. They can't take away our right to drink a perfectly normal beverage." Tyler was shouting now, his voice rising higher and higher in volume with every word.

"How am I supposed to stay awake and complete the millions of assignments they give us everyday?

I'm sure the government's argument will be, "Oh, just rest." But what they don't understand is that there is simply no time with the amount of work I have to do before college applications. I will die without coffee. It is literally my life. Does the government want an innocent kid to die because of their ridiculous law?

He was fuming, and if this was a cartoon, there would be literal smoke coming out of his ears. His ranting subsided as a bulb lit in his head. "You know what we should do? We should have online protests and open a caffeine speakeasy. I'm sure there are millions of other people who drink coffee in the US–they would definitely be patrons! And they can't do anything if millions of people are on our side, it is a democracy after all. We can be the country's knights in shining armour, saving the population from having to give up coffee."

"You know," Mrs. Bailey said, pondering, "That's actually not a bad idea. We have that shop down the street anyway. It's in perfect condition so we wouldn't have to repair it or anything. Why not use it to open a speakeasy?"

Mr. Bailey mentioned, "Yeah. We could keep it clandestine, only telling people that we know would support us, and asking the people who come to do the same." He was audibly becoming exuberant at the idea of doing something, anything at this point.

"We would also have to keep it very inconspicuous so government officials aren't alerted. Oh, and name the shop something generic," Tyler added, a smile breaking out on his face at the idea of forming a resistance.

"Come on. Let's go down there and start cleaning up. I'm sure it needs some dusting and sweeping, considering it's been shut for so long. The sooner we get this done, the sooner we can open it."

That's how Tyler found himself, an hour later, scrubbing the filthy wooden floors of their shop. Even as his hands ached, he reminded himself that they were doing something to fight this ridiculous law. That kept him going. As he was scrubbing a particular corner by the bookshelf, he noticed a faint golden glow around what looked like an ancient Greek letter carved into the floor. Carefully, he reached his hand out, fingertips trembling, and brushed his palm against the marking. The glow flared abruptly, then dimmed once again. Tyler frowned. What had happened? He pondered over it for another minute, then shrugged and continued to clean.

Unbeknownst to the Bailey family, the shop had just become invisible to passersby. Only the people they invited inside would be able to see it. Any government officials would just believe it was a derelict shop that had been abandoned.

The Bailey family spent their Saturday there—scrubbing, washing and dusting—to make the place habitable. After the labour portion of the afternoon was completed, they brought their vast collection of coffee makers that they had lying around at home (discreetly obviously, in several backpacks and tote bags), and set them up all around the room.

Mrs. Bailey brought her collection of antique vases, carefully handpicking which ones she would place. Tomorrow, they'd start inviting people—all coffee aficionados like them.

The first people they invited were Mrs. Bailey's brother and his family. They were more than happy to stop by. They invited close friends of theirs, who invited more of their own friends. The web, which had started out as just the Bailey family, a single point in the centre, continued to spread until all of these people were interconnected by their shared love for the elusive java bean.

As their speakeasy continued to grow, Mr. Bailey did wonder how they hadn't had any government intervention, but dismissed the thought, telling himself that they had just been lucky. Mrs. Bailey wasn't so optimistic. She, guessing that it was suspicious, brought it up with her family that night.

"Guys, have you noticed anything weird about the fact that no unwelcome visitors have accidentally meandered in since we started this in June?" It was now December.

"Yeah, I wondered that a few weeks ago too, but I thought we were just lucky," Mr. Bailey responded, his brow furrowed. "Now that I think about it though, it is weird. We should've had some close calls, but we haven't. Tyler, have you noticed anything?"

"Actually, yeah, now that I think about it," Tyler muttered slowly, "in June, when I was scrubbing the floor, I saw this engraved marking on the floor that was glowing golden. I touched it, and nothing happened, so I forgot about it. But now I'm thinking if that had something to do with this?"

That afternoon, Tyler showed them the glowing ancient Greek letter that had previously puzzled him. As his father's fingers touched it, a ripple went through the entire room, almost like a force field had lifted.

"This is what happened that day!" Mrs. Bailey cried. "Grandpa Joe made me promise to keep the property in our possession for as long as I could. He insisted I never sell this place after he died. I thought he just loved it, but obviously he knew about its impenetrability." She smiled a jubilant smile.

"Quick. Quick. Touch it again so we go back to being invisible!" Tyler exclaimed.

Mr. Bailey complied and the glow surrounding the carving flared once again, hiding them from view.

That was the story of a coffee-loving family that opened a #CaffeineSpeakeasy, which grew in popularity until almost all of America stood up for them. They rebelled together until coffee in tetra packs (to prevent the President from choking on coffee beans) was legalised. They still run their speakeasy today, as a tribute to the old times and to share their story.

A Second Chance

On a frosty winter night, Louise Williams was curled up in her favourite armchair by the comforting warmth of the fire. She held her fairytale open on her lap as she contemplated the beautiful ending that had warmed her heart. That was saying something, considering that she was eighty three years old. Not many things could move her anymore. As a particularly chilly gust blew in through her open window, she shivered violently, getting up at once to close it. Hurrying to the kitchen, she decided she was in the mood for tea with a hint of lemon and ginger, just the way she liked it.

As she was waiting for the tea to boil, she deeply inhaled the earthy aroma of the Darjeeling leaves that had been a gift from her neighbour. She noticed a cabinet that she had not touched for years, covered in dust with its paint peeling off. She did not know what quite possessed her to go over and look inside it today, but she moved towards it anyway. There were cobwebs hanging from the top most shelf due to disuse over the years. Apart from that, it was empty. There had not been anything inside of it for about twenty years now, not since her beloved husband had died. This space was where his favourite snacks had been kept, and it felt wrong to use it. In her mind, it seemed to almost tarnish his memory.

She gazed at it with nostalgia once more, examining it thoroughly. As she inspected it, she suddenly noticed a plain white envelope at the far end of the shelf. She hurriedly picked it up, her mind immediately wandering to conclusions as to what was inside and how it was there. Could her husband have left it here before he died? No, that was impossible. He had died in a freak car accident. She remembered that fateful day. It had been dark and silent. Louise and her husband Richard had been parked at the side of the road trying to look for Louise's lost earring when a driver slammed into them.

Richard died instantly, killed on impact, while Louise had broken a few bones. All she recollected from that horrendous day was a haze of panicked voices before she passed out, waking up in the hospital the next day. She had dissolved into tears upon being told her husband had been killed. Awful, gut-wrenching sobs had been dragged out of her as she mourned his loss.

The water boiled, snapping her out of her waking nightmare and back to reality. She tore open the envelope, finding a neatly written letter. Her heart sank as she stared at the handwriting that was not Richard's. It was silly, but she had held out a tiny bit of hope that it was from him. Still, she read the strange letter, not being able to make sense of it.

At the end, it said, "PS: say 'Trina'." That had been her mother's name.

Although she was discombobulated, she spoke the single word aloud tentatively.

Abruptly, she was jerked off her feet and spun around. All around her, she could see her life whizzing by, but it stopped in a particular time period, on her wedding day. She was astounded and bewildered as she took in the scene. It seemed the older version of herself had been brought back in time, and she now inhabited the body of her younger self. She spotted her now smooth skin, unlike the skin that was marred with wrinkles, causing it to sag. Her mobility improved, she could walk so much quicker, even maybe run. These changes thrilled her as she felt almost invincible.

As the realisation hit, a smile of complete and utter incredulity graced her mouth. She didn't question it, didn't ask 'why' or 'how.' Instead, she just thanked her lucky stars that she had been given this chance once more. Louise Williams went out to be married for the second time, to the same man, more rapturous than ever before.

This day was an exact replica of her original wedding day and Louise looked around in awe. There lay the gold and silver balloons that Richard had spent hours blowing up and arranging into a decorative archway just outside the door. She had been panicking, wondering how on earth they were going to pull this wedding together. Richard had soothed her, telling her to go to bed and not to worry, that he would take care of everything. Sure enough, she had woken the next day to see an archway completely made of those golden and silver balloons that she loved so much. It was shoddy at best, but she loved him for trying. Richard was passed out on the tiled floor of their living room, next to some unfilled balloons. His blond hair stuck up in tufts and his glasses were askew, sliding down his nose. She had reached out, fixed his glasses, smoothed down his hair, and left him to his dreams.

A soft voice in her ear brought her out of her reverie, and she started, blinking and focusing on the scene in front of her once again to find the source of the voice. Tears filled her eyes as she realised who it was, and she beamed a watery smile full of remembrance and renewed hope. A face she had not seen anywhere except in her memories in the last thirty years suddenly looked very much alive. The pallid demeanour and wide, lifeless eyes that had haunted her were replaced with rosy-tinted cheeks and twinkling eyes that were bright with jubilation. Louise was ecstatic that she had gotten a brief moment with her mother. She remembered when she had caught chickenpox, her mother had sat by her bedside all night as she tossed and turned, stroking her hair as she had tried to sleep. Her mother had always been her rock—the person who had stood by her side and supported her no matter what, so her death had hit hard. For nearly two years she was grief-stricken, a ghost of her former self, simply going through the motions of life. The joy that had been so easily discerned by her dancing eyes was extinguished. It seemed death had stolen the laughter and light in her life at the same moment it had claimed her mother's soul. This was a blessing, this one last day she had been given. An ultimate gift from the universe, maybe even from her mother, who'd blessed her from her grave.

Her mother's soft voice wrapped her in a cocoon of love and warmth as she stated simply, "I'm so proud of you Louise, you know that right?" Overcome with emotion, she merely nodded, her eyes conveying the words she could not speak. Her mother beamed another radiant smile, squeezed Louise's hand and walked away.

Then, she saw him. Her vision tunnelled and the hubbub around her faded, as he looked straight at her and grinned, his pure joy lighting up his eyes until they sparkled. He looked dashing in his black tuxedo. Louise had forgotten what he looked like in formal attire, his preferred choice of clothing being t-shirts and jeans. The black brought out his tan and made his eyes seem bigger, their turquoise colour even more vivid. She gazed back, smiling so wide that she felt her face might have split open. She did not care. The unadulterated elation she experienced emanated a warm glow inside of her, expanding and touching every part of her body until her nerves were on fire; she was encased in a golden bubble rippling and swelling, fed by her sheer joy. No words existed to describe the relief and euphoria she experienced just by seeing his face for the first time in twenty years. The freak accident had stolen him from her, but now, finally, he was here, even if it was only for one night.

Looking down at herself, she noticed for the first time that she was in her old wedding dress, the one that had been her mother's. She hiked her skirts up, and as fast as she could in her supremely uncomfortable shoes, she ran towards him. All her life, she had run towards him, and would continue to do so at every opportunity, so great was her love. Richard turned towards her once more, spotted her haphazard form darting in his direction and held his arms out.

She crashed into them and squeezed him tightly, relishing his solid form. She felt his laugh reverberating in the air around her, his chest shaking with the force of his mirth. She just shook her head and smiled, squeezing her eyes shut and dusting off her old memories. She placed a snapshot of this moment glittering with renewed hope, right next to all the times she had shared with Richard.

He leaned down to whisper to her, "Ready to get married?" He could not know that they had been married once already and that they had shared this almost tangible bond.

Even so, once was not enough, she needed eternity. But she would settle for one last time. So, she nodded vigorously. She had not been more sure of anything in her life. She told him so, and he twinkled his blinding smile, the one that was reserved for her and only her.

She gripped him tightly, wanting to hold onto this moment for as long as possible, knowing that when nightfall came, she, like Cinderella, would be transported to her own reality. As bittersweet as it was, she sighed contentedly. This was exactly what she had wished for all those lonely years, and it had finally been granted.

She danced the night away with her lost love and felt like the luckiest woman alive. And when it was time for her to go, she hugged her Richard one last time, told him she loved him forever and made her way down the glass staircase and to her own soon-to-be pumpkin carriage.

Binding Shackles

I felt trapped. Suffocated. The walls slowly closed in around me until I could barely draw in a shuddering breath. My fingers itched to pick up my guitar, but I couldn't. I had to write this essay first. Books lay scattered across every surface, all my music sheets tucked into far corners. I never had the time to work on my music anymore, I was always so busy with my courses. I knew that I was privileged and lucky in a way most kids could never hope to be. I was at one of the best universities in the US, but my dream was to become an artist, the musical kind, not the art kind (I couldn't draw to save my life). I'd performed at a few small places before. Whenever I was on stage, everything else was nonexistent. Every worry and every fear left my mind as the music-induced haze of the beat pulsing and the energy of the crowd took over. Instead of doing what made me happy, I was here, at the University of Michigan, getting a degree in business that I didn't want. It was so mundane, there was no uniqueness or creativity that went into it. There were no bright hues in my future, just shades of black and white that threatened to throttle me.

Everyday was the same. Eat, study, sleep, repeat. Some days, there wasn't even enough time to sleep. I was drowning in my course load, each book reaching its spindly arms out, choking me. I knew I would have loved it at Julliard. I'd even gotten an acceptance. I remembered that day, sitting on my bed in my pajamas, refreshing the page every minute, waiting for it to update. The ecstatic feeling in my chest as I read the words 'Congratulations…' This same joy had buoyed me all the way down the stairs and into the kitchen to announce to my father that I had applied, even gotten in. But my father hadn't let me go, said that music wouldn't give me a stable life and that it was a dead end. I'd believed him then, eager to gain his approval, and thrown the letter out, instead accepting the University of Michigan's offer. I hadn't known how wrong I was. I wasn't cut out for this life, a life of drab walls and desks and glass offices, a lifetime of suits and ties and shirts, and meaningless presentations. I wanted to be free. I wanted a life of tours and sold-out stadiums, my music pounding through the speakers, lifting me up, high on adrenaline.

This degree was slowly wringing my neck, and that wasn't a cost that was worth it.

I sighed, burying my head under my pillows. Tomorrow. I decided I would drop out to focus on my music. My parents weren't supportive.

I was constantly told, "Music isn't stable" and "You won't earn enough money." They thought I should get a degree, sit behind a desk all day, and earn lots of money to support my future family. But I couldn't take it anymore. For as long as I could remember, this had been my dream, but I'd always been pushed into doing things I didn't want to. Tomorrow morning would be the last time I ever set foot in this place. With my mind made up resolutely, I rolled over and fell asleep as my head finally stopped spinning.

The next morning, there was still a moment of lingering hesitation, a pinprick of self-doubt asking me if I was really doing the right thing. But no. It was time to go. This decision was mine to make. The years I'd spent here came back to me. It hadn't been all bad. There were some moments of light in the darkness. I'd made some amazing friends here, friends who had supported me when my own parents hadn't. This ending was bittersweet, but it was time to begin a new chapter in my life. As I'd decided the night before, I packed up my things, took one last look at the dorm that had been my home for three years and left. As soon as I was out of those believed-to-be hallowed walls, I could breathe easier. For the first time in years, I had a spring in my step and the weight of the world was mostly off my shoulders. The tiny bit that was left to do was call my parents and tell them that I was out of this place for good. I didn't know how they would react—well, actually I did. They'd be mad at me and tell me that I was throwing away an opportunity of a lifetime. But I'd be throwing away my talents if I didn't at least *try* to follow my dream. I owed myself that much.

The first thing I did was sit in a coffee shop with all my song ideas. I then proceeded to write. Now that the ball of anxiety about business school had mostly dissipated, lyrics just poured out of me. I had too many ideas and not enough hands to write them all down. Anything that my gaze landed on, lyrics would pop into my head. Lyrics that didn't need refining; they hadn't come this easy to me in a long time. Words swirled around in my head, and I tried to remember them long enough to put them down on the piece of paper in front of me. I didn't know how long I sat there, filling napkins with lyrics, composing melodies, lost in my own uncomplicated world of chords and crochets. This had been my escape from the start, my happy place; it was what I loved to do. I couldn't let the opinions of others take it away from me.

I had put it off for long enough, but it was probably time to call my parents. The joy drained out of me at that thought, but I still dug into my backpack for my phone. My dad picked up on the first ring, and I put him on hold while I added my mom to the call. "So," I started hesitantly, "I have something to tell you."

"What is it, sweetie?" my mother asked, sounding concerned.

In a rush, I said, "I dropped out of university to focus on my music."

"What? Can you say that again? I didn't quite catch it." This was my father, his voice gruff.

My stomach was in knots. I took a deep breath in, trying to calm my racing nerves. I said, slower this time, "I dropped out of university to focus on my music." Loud, indignant voices exploded into my ear in protest. I closed my eyes, disconnected the call and threw my head back onto the seat, hard. I didn't know why I was so upset. It wasn't like I expected them to be supportive of this decision. But it still hurt. I guess a tiny part of me thought they would be understanding. But my engineer parents couldn't be. They wanted me to do something worthwhile, as they called it, with my life. They didn't like the fact that I had different ambitions. But I would prove them wrong by making a name for myself in music. I knew I would.

Fate? Maybe Destiny?

"No! Please!" I cried, begging the flight attendant. "Let me board. I'm sorry I'm late, but I have a really important job interview. Please!" She remained resolute, a grim expression painted on her face. I widened my eyes, trying my hardest to let a few tears leak out in imitation of my best look of innocence. I could see her hard exterior cracking, the exact moment when she decided to take pity on me.

"Okay, fine. But I'm recording this. It can't happen again."

"Absolutely. Thank you so much!" I dashed towards the ramp connecting the airport to the plane, dragging my suitcase behind me.

"Okay, 24C. 24C." I mumbled under my breath, frantically scanning the row numbers. There it was. I shoved my luggage into the overhead compartment, before quickly sitting down. As I settled in my seat, a particular face tugged at the edges of my memory. I squinted my eyes and looked closely, trying to recollect. The blonde hair, the curve of her nose and the sharp lines of her cheekbones all tickled my brain, as it persistently tried to recognise this familiar yet unfamiliar face. I stared at her for a few more seconds, the few extra seconds perhaps bordering on stalkerish territory, because she looked at me in bewilderment, maybe even a little bit of fear. Abruptly, it clicked. "Lina?" I asked incredulously. She turned around in surprise. Now that I could see her clearly, there was no doubt in my mind that it was her.

"Anne? Wh-How are you here?" She stuttered. "I have a job interview in Chicago," I said.

"Ah, cool," she responded. She nodded, then turned back to continue staring out the window. It was a clear indication that she didn't want to talk to me. Intense sorrow washed over me as I looked over at her; all the times we'd spent together came back to me in a cascading wave. The time I'd broken my leg climbing a tree when we were eight, and Lina had covered for me, saying I'd tripped on the edge of the sidewalk. She'd refused to leave my side, hanging onto my arm all the way to the hospital, her face pinched and white with worry. Her nails had left angry red half-moon crescents on my arm that refused to fade. I think she'd been in more pain than I was. I'd always been the reckless one and she the worrier, our personalities balancing each other out perfectly. There was a time when we were older, maybe around fourteen, and we'd stay up all night just talking and laughing, eating sweets and drinking hot chocolate as midnight snacks. Lina often fell asleep with her head on my shoulder, and I'd look down at her and think, "This is what pure friendship feels like." I remember feeling this overwhelming elation that consumed me as I fully comprehended that thought. I asked her if we were best friends, and she replied without a second thought, "Of course, why would you think any differently?" In that moment, we grinned at each other, and a bond that could never be severed had been formed between us. Or, so I thought. As time went by, our long chats turned into brief texts. It became more apparent than I preferred. We were drifting apart. Before knowing it, five years had passed and neither one of us had tried to contact the other. I was ready to leave the past behind and move on; I hoped she was too. Because truth be told, I had missed her, as much as I'd tried to deny it. But I couldn't just say these things to her face, there were too many scars from our past, scars that had held us apart all those years ago, and scars that threatened to continue to distance us now.

How do you say that to someone who's practically a stranger to you now, even if you had known them better than anybody in the past? I didn't know. So, I swallowed thickly, suppressing all the words I had wanted to say for five years, words it looked like I wouldn't ever have a chance to say. I looked over at Lina, experiencing inexplicable sorrow for the time that we had wasted, neither of us knowing better. After that, it had been too difficult to reach out, having memories of those childish acts, the petty high school drama that had wedged us apart. I couldn't really blame her if she hated me. Images from our past played over and over in my head like a broken record. Images of downcast expressions, unshed tears glittering, a few spilling over, racing past each other. Images of the pain etched on both of our faces, the dark circles under our eyes, the chasm of unsaid words between us taking their toll.

I sighed, and sunk down low in my seat, not wanting to look in Lina's direction and see the utter lack of emotion on her face. I put my headphones in and closed my eyes, sleep sinking its claws into me and dragging me under the surface. I woke up what felt like minutes later to a loud voice crackling over the PA system. I rubbed my eyes and sat up, trying to discern the words that were being repeated. I glanced sideways and saw that Lina had her eyes shut tightly and was gripping the armrests with such force that her knuckles had turned white. I suddenly remembered she was afraid of turbulence. I contemplated letting it go, but my conscience wouldn't allow me to do so. Against my better judgement, I leaned over and gripped her hand. Her eyes flew wide open and she stared at me as her eyes glittered with unshed tears. I continued to be her anchor, keeping her fear at bay. She curled her fingers around mine and shut her eyes once more, her death grip on the armrests relaxing ever so slightly. I fell back into my dreamless haze, still clutching Lina's hand.

A few hours later, I was awakened by something brushing against my legs. I blinked my eyes open blearily and discovered it was Lina trying to get past me to go to the toilet. I sat up quickly, moving my long legs aside so she could pass. I examined her closely for the first time, noticing little details that had changed about her. All traces of baby fat had left her face, sharpening her high cheekbones and fashioning a pronounced jawline. But there had been a light in her eyes, a light that had blazed like twin suns fabricated with hope and joy, a light that had now winked out, leaving hollow, depthless pools in its wake. She averted her gaze as soon as she saw me looking. This made me inexplicably upset. I didn't know why. I told myself perhaps I should stop caring. But that was the problem - I couldn't. I hadn't known it then, but the absence of my best friend had hurt like the loss of a limb, a limb I wasn't willing to give up. Our friendship hadn't been perfect, far from it actually, but I was willing to fight for it. What we had was special, the kind of bond that was extremely rare. The kind of bond that however frayed, however thin, couldn't ever fully be snapped. We were oceans away from each other, but I was prepared to swim towards her, and I was betting Lina was too. This strengthened my resolve, and I decided I would at least talk to her once she came back.

Once she was settled in her seat, I said hesitantly, "Hey Lina?" She reluctantly turned towards me. "Can we leave what happened between us behind? Because I really missed you in university. Remember how we had that plan to live in an apartment together?" She smiled at that, albeit a little hesitantly. But I would take it. The fact that she was even willing to acknowledge me was heartening. "Instead of you, I had to live with someone else from university. It wasn't nearly as much fun as we could have had. I needed my best friend to know me, to let me be me and to support me," I said. She let out a slight snort at that.

"Oh, you can't possibly mean that. I didn't support you. Instead, I tried to drag you down just because I was jealous. What kind of best friend does that?" she said.

"It's okay. Everyone gets jealous. True, we both could have handled it better, but I forgive you. I just want you back in my life," I responded, my eyes brimming with emotion. She had tears in her eyes and a disbelieving smile on her face. I grinned back, my throat feeling thick. I felt a golden glow expanding in my chest, warming my body from the inside out, as ecstasy held me as an obliging prisoner.

We hugged each other, tightly, never wanting to let go again. The rest of the five-hour flight was spent amiably, chatting and laughing, catching up on all the years we had missed in each other's lives.

"Wait, why are you going to Chicago?" I asked curiously.

"Oh, job interview," she said. Clutching each other, we both let out laughs full of pure joy. Nothing would come between us again. I would make sure of it. This moment was the happiest I had been in a long time, and I didn't plan on doing anything that would ruin that, at least not again.

Elevators: Awkward, Am I Right?

*I*n a flurry of movement, Annalise grabbed her purse, checked for her keys and rushed out of the house, her long dark hair swinging behind her. She slammed the door shut in her haste and jammed her finger on the elevator button, praying for its quick arrival. She couldn't be late to this job interview. Living on the seventy second floor was both a blessing and a curse. Cars and people all looked minuscule from the top, almost as if they were in a miniature dollhouse. But the elevator always took forever to show up, stopping at what seemed like twenty floors before it arrived at hers. It was frustrating, having to wait that long everyday. It seemed like she spent half of her life waiting for it, her heeled black pumps resting in the same spot on the maroon linoleum floor.

Everyday she desperately prayed that the elevator would remain empty, and everyday her prayers were ignored. It appeared that the universe constantly wanted to push her out of her admittedly tiny comfort zone. She absolutely despised awkward elevator rides with strangers. The anxiety of never knowing what to say, or even *if* she was supposed to say anything sent her brain reeling and into overdrive, each thought louder than the last. Her palms started to sweat, and she began tapping her foot to a constant rhythm that was inaudible to anyone but her. Sometimes shivers overtook her body and goosebumps rose on her skin, the hair on her arms standing straight up. In an attempt to dissuade overly enthusiastic strangers from talking to her, she always kept her eyes on the floor and her arms crossed, yet they never seemed to take the hint. Time in that metal can felt insignificant. Even when she was there for a minute or two, it felt like she'd been in the elevator for hours. Maybe it was to do with her desire to escape, or maybe the elevator was a mysterious place in which time didn't exist.

A sudden *ding* brought her back to reality. She glanced up to see that the elevator had finally arrived, and sure enough, her streak of bad luck continued as she peered in to find a man standing at the far end of the elevator. A split-second decision had her stepping foot onto the carpeted floor with a reluctant sigh, not wanting to wait for a second elevator and risk that being occupied too. Okay, she could make this work.

Hopefully.

The glass doors swung shut behind her, and she turned her attention to the man. He was entirely focused on the newspaper in his hand, and she took the opportunity to covertly study him. It was like she'd walked onto the street during a typical, gloomy English thunderstorm. He wore a dark grey tweed coat over a shirt that was a slightly lighter shade of his grey than his coat. His trousers were also loose and grey. What a shocker, Annalise thought. His grey hair was immaculately combed and he wore a heavy, expensive-looking watch on his right wrist. The only thing about him that wasn't grey was his skin, and that could have been too. He could have camouflaged with the grey walls if it wasn't for the bold, black letters on his newspaper, Annalise thought. His face was a blank wall, wiped of any expression, not even a single telltale sign of his emotions. He looked like the sort of man who was hardly living, just existing in life. He seemed to have no joy at all, and he seemed blissfully unaware of it.

As it stopped on another floor; the elevator *dinged* yet again. Another man sashayed in and Annalise did a double take. Then, she groaned internally. She really hoped this one wouldn't try to talk to her, though she wasn't optimistic. He seemed like the sort of person who would make conversation with anyone. Bright pink pants were slung low on his hips. His shirt was dark blue and he had a top hat. The spikes of his hair were dyed a striking pink on one side and a dark blue on the other; each spike was perfected with glitter. To top it all off, a magenta feather boa was draped over him, with the ends trailing along behind him on the ground. He stood tall, with his spine straight and chin lifted up, his stance oozing confidence. He had a bubbly smile and the sort of charisma that would attract people, a perfect example of an extreme extrovert.

It was interesting, Annalise thought, how many completely different types of people there were in the world. There were two standing right in front of her who were polar opposites. A sudden loud clearing of a throat shocked her out of her contemplation and she started. The man who was covered in grey from head to toe spoke.

"So, I'm sure you're all wondering why I've gathered you here," he said, before hitting the emergency stop button on the elevator console. Annalise's eyes widened for a split second, the motion only half completed before everything went black.

Puppets in a Cage

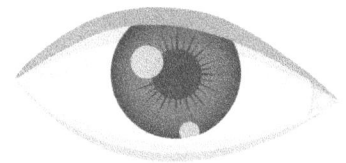

Don't tell them you can see.
Don't tell them you can see

Cars honking, weaving through rush hour traffic. Unbothered pedestrians continuing on their path to the subway, occasionally dodging a car here and there. Billboards flashing neon, advertising some new product. It was just another conventional day in Manhattan.

Carlos was walking back home from work, taking the shortcut through the alleyways he always used. They stank so badly that he felt like he would double over and puke all over his shoes, but they saved him a good ten minutes. So, he continued to use them, stomaching the foetid odour everyday.

As usual, the slap of his leather shoes on the granite echoed through the small, dimly lit space; the sound was now as familiar to him as the back of his hand. The emotions in his thoughts set the pace for the beat of his footsteps, distracting him from the stench.

Today, he was angry. It had been an especially atrocious day. First, his boss had screamed at him for being two minutes late when he was delayed all the time.

"Hypocrite," Carlos muttered under his breath. Shortly after, someone had spilled coffee all over his desk, ruining all his important papers. Finally, on the way back, he'd stepped in a puddle of pee which seemed extremely acidic because it had completely burned through his brand new brown leather shoes.

All he wanted was to get home, shower, and curl up in his favourite armchair by the window with a new mystery in hand.

His reverie was rudely disturbed as he passed an especially disgusting stretch where multiple trash cans overflowed with a kind of slimy concoction. He hurriedly plugged his nose as he retched violently, the reek too revolting for even him—a veteran—to stand.

Carlos was beyond questioning it. You never questioned what had happened on the streets of New York. He quickened his pace considerably, breathing in a sigh of relief once he was no longer inhaling the stench - well, no more than usual.

He continued to hurry through, consoled by the fact that he was almost home. Lost in his own thoughts, his gaze fixed on his own constant footsteps, he didn't notice the darkness that had befallen the city. It was only when the red brick coated with graffiti around him started to blur, did he look up to the sky. There was no sun. It was like it had never existed at all. But that wasn't possible, since it was the middle of the day. As Carlos gazed upwards in disbelief; black spots started to dance across his vision. His breath came fast, in short pants. His hands started to shake violently, his blood pounding in his ears, heart thudding in his chest. "Breathe in. Breathe out." He felt goosebumps rise on his arms, the hair there standing up straight. "Breathe in." The quality of his eyesight was deteriorating quickly. He blinked frantically, trying to clear his vision, but nothing worked. Everything was blurring, slowly fading away. Within the next minute, it was gone, fallen into the welcoming arms of darkness.

He felt helpless. If he couldn't see, he couldn't do anything. With his back to the wall, Carlos slid down, until he was sitting on the ground in the disgusting alleyway with his head in his hands. He felt warm tears slide down his cheeks as his heart began to pound even faster. His body trembled with the effort of trying to hold back his sobs. He screamed, clawing desperately at the wall behind him, scraping the soft skin of his palms raw in the process. Blood welled from the gashes. He didn't understand. What had happened? How could someone with perfect 20/20 vision suddenly lose their eyesight? That wasn't normal, right? He leaned his head against the brick wall behind him, the impact echoing through the stillness.

What Carlos didn't know was that it wasn't just him, the whole city of New York had gone blind within the span of five minutes. It was like life had come to a halt. Everything was silent, not a single sound to be heard. The silence was unnatural, eerie. It was like glass had fallen over the city, separating it from the rest of the world. New York was in its own little bubble, unmoving, while life continued as normal everywhere else.

Nothing moved or breathed, as if a button had been pushed and all existence had responded to the command, simply going to sleep. For two years, the city of New York sat in its ghostly tranquility, puppets in a glass cage.

TWO YEARS LATER

Though they didn't know it, today was the day there would be hustling and bustling on the streets of New York once more. Today was the day the city would finally awaken from its lengthy slumber. Whatever entity had done this, today they were finally going to take pity on the city, blowing new animation into the empty shells that were once sparked with life.

Carlos opened his eyes, unknown to him, but for the first time in two years. To the ones that had slept, it had only felt like two hours. He was still in the alleyway where he'd lost his vision. As he remembered that, the overwhelming stench hit him all over again. He retched, his body spasming, but he managed not to vomit. As Carlos shook his head from side to side, he noticed that his vision was starting to develop again. He could make out hazy pinpricks of colour all around him. As he squeezed his eyes shut, it came back in full force, dazing him. His head hit the wall once again. After he'd adjusted, he marvelled at the fact that he could see again, drinking in all the details of the world.

Glancing around, he noticed what looked a lot like text scrawled on every surface.

Examining it closely, he discerned that it was the same thing written over and over again, in every available font, in every possible size. The script looked hastily scrawled, the words glowing a golden glow, almost leaking light.

It said, "Don't tell them you can see."

I Have a Heart to Heart With My Great-Great-Great-Grandmother

*D*isgruntled, Lina had been clicking the keys on her laptop impatiently for the past hour. When that hadn't worked, she'd switched to pacing restlessly along the length of her fuzzy carpet, almost wearing a hole into it. She was trying to think of a stellar idea that would blow everyone away, but it was *not* going well, to put it in the mildest terms. She had been attempting to write a novel for weeks now and she *still* hadn't gotten anywhere. Trying to think of a new, original idea was harder than it seemed. It seemed like all of the ideas in the world had been used up. Whenever she thought she'd finally got it, she would search it up and there would already be something published based on the idea. To say it was frustrating was saying the least. Lina didn't understand what the problem was. She'd been an amazing writer all her life; all her teachers had told her she would be a successful author one day. After all, Jane Austen *had* been her great-great-great-grandmother. Writing ran in her blood. But maybe the skill in her blood was diluted after so many generations. At this rate, Lina was never going to be like her late grandmother. Since she was old enough to talk, her lifelong dream had been to be a best-selling author one day.

Every university had been impressed by the finesse of her writing. The way she could craft words, using them to her advantage was truly outstanding. But now that her dream was riding on her talent, she couldn't do it. She couldn't master her skill and hone it to write a novel that would blow everyone away. Shutting her eyes angrily, she leaned back heavily in her chair, feeling defeated. She could practically see her aspirations crumbling down around her, fracturing over and over again until they were nothing but jagged fragments.

She sighed heavily, banging the back of her head against the soft leather of her chair, in hopes that it would help her jump-start her overused brain. It didn't help. Likely, it just scrambled her cognitive cells. But at this point who cared? It's not like she was able to come up with anything before. She rubbed her eyes, hoping it would get rid of some of the itchiness and she'd be able to think clearly, coming up with a brilliant idea in a genius stroke of inspiration. But no. Nothing. Of course, there was nothing. She didn't even know why she bothered anymore. Except this was how she'd get to university. While brilliant, her family didn't have a lot of money. Not to sound harsh, but they were all failed writers trying to live up to their ancestor, Jane Austen's, unbeatable legacy. Her grandfather had tried to write a book about a boy with anxiety, which hadn't sold. There probably wasn't a market for that sort of book back then. Her father had written one about a high school janitor who tries to enact revenge on the students who made his life difficult. None of these had been successful. All of the pressure was on her. The weight of all these expectations threatened to break her. She knew how it felt to be second best, to be constantly overshadowed no matter what she did. They couldn't afford to send her to university, her only option was a scholarship, which didn't seem very imminent if she continued at this rate.

Through her closed eyelids, she saw a warm golden glow expanding beside her. It radiated warmth, the very essence of pure elation. As she peeled her eyes open in confusion, she saw a ghostly apparition next to her. She startled, knocking her elbow into the edge of her desk. Rubbing it ruefully to soothe the sharp pain, she glanced up. She squinted, trying to make out the woman's features. She had the same naturally curly brunette hair as Lina, the same hazel eyes, and the same rich complexion. She was tall and slender, matching Lina's figure perfectly. As it clicked, she gasped. "Y-you, are you Jane Austen? My great-great-great-grandmother?" The woman, Jane, nodded, a gentle smile gracing her lips.

"I am. I've seen you struggling these past few weeks, but I didn't want to come down here too early. I wanted to make sure you actually needed my help."

Lina was still absolutely stunned that she was talking to *the* Jane Austen, but at the mention of her failed novel, she looked straight at her grandmother and implored, "Please help me. Anything you think will make a difference. How did you write *Pride and Prejudice* or *Sense and Sensibility*? I can't think of a single distinctive idea. I've been trying so hard for weeks and weeks but it's just not coming to me," she wailed.

At that, Lina's grandmother smiled. "My dear child, I wrote what I wanted to write, what was in my heart of hearts. Even though they may not know it, there is always a hidden passion in an author's heart. Trust me. There is something you want to write about, but you haven't explored it yet. A best-selling book comes from honesty and sincerity.

Readers resonate with you if you're able to do that. And I know you can. You are a remarkable author," she said encouragingly.

Some of the light entered Lina's eyes once again but quickly dimmed after a self-deprecating thought. "I want to follow in your footsteps, but what if I'm not good enough? What if all I manage to do is disappoint you?"

"Dear Lina, you could never. I am always proud of you, whatever you do. I will still be proud of you if you decide tomorrow that you want to be a marine biologist instead." "Thank you, Grandma." Lina really was grateful, but sometimes, during the darkest of nights, she thought it would have been better to not be related to a legend. It would make her life so much easier, allowing her room to breathe. Everyone wouldn't expect perfection. She could just be a normal author, finding her voice and improving her skills with every piece she wrote. She could grow as a person, her experiences fueling her writing. Since her grandma was actually here, it would be better to air out her petty grievances than to brood over them shamefully.

So, mustering up her courage, she blurted it out. Her grandmother listened intently, lips curved into a sad smile. "It's okay Lina," she said.

Worried that she'd upset her grandmother, Lina backtracked. "I still admire you and your talent, and of course I love you. Sometimes I just feel small, like I couldn't be anything compared to you."

"Don't worry. You're much better than I ever was. I have no doubt you'll write the next great novel that will live forever in people's hearts. I will be known as Lina Austen's grandmother soon enough, I'm sure of it."

Lina's smile broke free, and she grinned broadly. "Thank you, Grandma." Her grandmother nodded her head, smiling wistfully down at her granddaughter.

Abruptly, her grandma's form began to flicker around the edges, the golden glow shrinking. "Goodbye Lina. I have to go now. I'm not allowed to stay very long, but I promise I will visit you soon." Within the blink of an eye, she vanished and it was like she'd never been here in the first place.

She would try brainstorming again tomorrow, but the beginnings of an idea had started to take root in her mind. A very real story inspired by her own life that came from a place close to her heart, just like her grandma had said. For now, all she wanted to do was to eat some ice cream and take a nice, long nap and so she did just that, waiting for her lightning bolt of inspiration to fully strike.

The Book of History

"James. JAMES!" I jolted awake, frantically sitting up. As my sleep-crusted eyelids peeled open, Mr. Madison's death glare, directed straight at me, came into view. "Sorry sir," I apologised. He glared at me some more, then snorted and walked away, disgusted.

"As I've been asking you for five minutes, how did World War I begin?" He had a sweet smile plastered on his face, but I knew that he was crowing with delight on the inside.

"I - I don't know sir."

He leered, "Of course you wouldn't! You clearly think my lessons are an appropriate time to take a nap." The saccharine-sweet smile again. "You are going to catch up on all the work you miss when you take naps, and write an essay about the origin of the two world wars. I want it on my desk first thing tomorrow morning."

That night, I sat on my bed cursing Mr. Miller, yet doing the work he'd demanded (the dude was scary, and his deceptively sweet smile sent chills down my back everytime). I opened my textbook and crossed out a sentence, feeling it was useless. I put my head into my hands, trying to think of a way to start this cursed essay. When nothing came to my mind, I banged the back of my head repeatedly against my leather chair, hoping it would knock some useful words into my brain. I tried to write something for a few more minutes, then gave up. I didn't want detention tomorrow, but it looked like I would be staying after school anyway, with Mr. Miller's death glare boring a hole in my back.

I started to doodle in the margins, drawing little people and shading them in. They looked life-like, each pencil stroke contributing to the careful myriad of lines that made up the images. Drawing was the only thing I was good at in school. My art teacher thought I was precocious; she said I had serious talent and that if I put in a bit more effort, I could make a career out of my art. As I watched, the ink I was drawing with started to fade. I groaned, rummaging around in my desk for a different pen and continuing to doodle. When that started to fade too, I flipped the page to look at the doodle I'd just done. There was nothing there. But that's where I'd drawn it. I was sure of it.

Flipping the page again, I watched as the ink that I'd just drawn in completely dissolved into the paper. I wrote 'hello' in the margin, and that disappeared too. What was happening? Where was the ink going? I shook the book, then stopped immediately, feeling stupid. Abruptly, I noticed writing on the corner of the page; it was a new scrawl, not something that was printed or something I had written. I squinted my eyes and bent so my eyes were closer to the page.

It said, "Hey. These doodles are really good."

I was absolutely confounded. It wasn't until a minute later that I shakily wrote back. "Thanks. Who are you?"

I waited until I started to see ink appear on the page, my heart thudding in my chest.

"I'm Matthew. What about you?" I couldn't believe it. I was communicating with someone through my history textbook. How was this possible?

Shaking my head in wonder, I replied, "James. I'm in California. Where are you?" I leaned back in my seat, almost holding my breath.

"New York. This is crazy. I've known that the ink disappears when I write in this textbook for months, but I didn't know that it worked almost like a walkie-talkie and that there was somebody with its twin.' I smiled. This was definitely unfathomable.

I replied, "That's so cool! I love the M&M store in Times Square."

"What? There is no M&M store…"

"What do you mean? I went to New York last summer on a school trip, I remember it being huge because Mr. Miller was so excited. It was hilarious to see my history teacher more excited by M&Ms than teenagers.'

"That is funny. But James, can you describe the Times Square you saw to me?"

"Yeah. There were flashing neon lights, billboards on skyscrapers and loads of people milling (no pun intended) about."

"In my world, there are small buildings and no neon lights"

"Wait…what year is it?"

"1941"

"WHAT?! It's 2022"

"Are we seriously communicating through time? This just got even crazier."

"Tell me about it."

This time, I tried writing, "Hitler says I'm an idiot and calls off the war." Before my eyes, the entire section about World War II vanished from my textbook. I was astonished. How did me writing that make the text fade away? Unless… No, that was impossible. Right? But there was no other explanation. I could also alter history. Simply by changing it in my school textbook. I was in shock. I had just written that to make Matthew laugh; I didn't think it would actually work. Who had decided to give an irresponsible kid like me a textbook with powers like these? They were a huge liability. But I could handle them. Probably. I hoped.

For the first time in my life, I was early to school the next morning. Also a first, I went straight to the library to pore over my textbook. There was so much I could do. I could erase all the wars and conflicts in history, achieving world peace. This thought drove me forwards and I barged straight in. The librarian gave me a weird glance because I was never in here; I always avoided the library like the plague. I ignored all the stares I was attracting and made a beeline for an empty corner table, sitting down and hurriedly pulling my textbook out of my bag. I started crossing out every line, absorbed in the strategic, yet repetitive task, disregarding the bell signalling I should get to class.

I glanced up at last, having erased the whole textbook, and nearly had a heart attack. The world was in ruins; everything around me was nothing more than rubble, shattered into little pieces. Shards of glass littered the streets, each piece creating a spectrum of colours every time a ray of light hit it. The buildings were gone, broken into a million hunks of cement that joined the wreckage on the streets. What had I done? Barely a day with the power and I'd destroyed the world. How could I have thought attaining world peace would be this easy? Of course it wasn't as simple and crossing out every line in a book. Our world and society were an amalgam of destruction and development. As two sides of a coin, they were inextricable. The worst horrors that our world had witnessed had catalysed some of the most inspiring, propulsive developments. So, it had to be really thought about. What parts could go and what had to stay so that the developments that had occurred in the world wouldn't be redacted too.

As a thought crossed my mind, I shot out of my seat and started to pace. I could fix this if I just rewrote what I had wiped out. Now, if I could just find the book... I gazed at the ruins around me desperately, trying to spot it. But just my luck, it seemed to have evanesced. In despair, I put my head in my hands and slumped in my seat. I guess I'd just have to live with the fact that I had demolished all of human kind.

But wait. Would I? What if I simply had an unexplainable bond with Matthew? What if it wasn't related to the textbook at all? I know that that's what he had told me, that we could communicate because of the book. But what if he was wrong? Fueled by this thought, I picked up one of the books littering my side and flipped it open to a random page. Scrambling for my pen, I wrote "HEY MATTHEW."

His reply was instantaneous, "What's up James?"

"So, a little bit of a problem, I kind of destroyed the world and I can't find the textbook to fix it."

"I noticed. Okay. So. Find a blank book and copy the textbook into it. I'll copy it out for you bit by bit so you can put it in the new book."

"Oh! Thank you so much." I was so relieved.

"Don't thank me yet. I don't know if this is going to work."

We got to work. I started to copy what Matthew was telling me exactly into the blank book I'd found. As I worked, I saw pieces start to reconstruct themselves, slowly threading together to become the objects they once were. It was working! I continued to tirelessly copy out what Matthew was writing for me, my hand cramping. I was so grateful for Matthew; he was helping me fix a mess he hadn't even made.

After several hours, I glanced up to see the sun setting, washing the sky in hues of apricot and crimson. The world was almost restored back to its original state; only a few shards of rubble remained. This had been an important lesson for me, a lesson to leave history as it was. I guess everything did happen for a reason, and I couldn't and shouldn't try to undo it. Instead, I should find a way to move forward and grow.

Death of the Sun

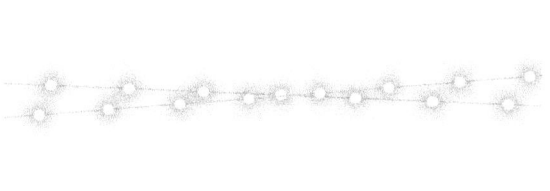 

*T*he repetitive *bang* of gunshots sounded, reverberating through the destroyed wasteland that had once been our world. Now, all that was left were dilapidated buildings and demolished hunks of metal that had once been cars. Roads that were previously smooth now had craters along them from the demons' earth-shattering footsteps. I was surrounded by hungry growls and pleading shrieks. I'd gotten so used to them over the past two weeks that I barely reacted at all. These noises of affliction and desolation had become a common occurrence in this world. A few weeks ago, millions of demons had descended onto Earth from a swirling blue portal that had abruptly opened up in the sky. Demons of all colours, shapes and sizes, each possessed a different deadly weapon.

The most destructive of them all was huge, with a serpentine body. It was jet black, darker than the darkest pits of hell. Scales tougher than any material on Earth covered its form. Without any warning, these creatures had torn through the streets, ravaging the world and causing mass panic and hysteria. People had tried to flee, but they'd been no match for these fiends. Each living thing had been picked off one by one and devoured until there was hardly anything left.

FIVE YEARS LATER

Today. Today was our last chance to rewrite the fate of any humanity left in this dystopian world. My gang and I were rebels, the few people remaining that refused to bow down to his orders. We chose our own path, trying to do good in this demolished world. It was so far gone that the sun was merely a blackened dead thing, not even a single ember remaining that could spark it to life. There was not a single leaf or blade of grass in sight. Everything good about the world, everything pure, had been ripped from it leaving nothing but the essence of evil, of sin at its heart. Over the last five years, we'd dubbed it *Resurgemus,* 'rise' in Latin, to remind us to oppose the threat. And today, we would finally do so. We would wrench the throne from his hands. He believed that humans were weak, scared creatures that would flee, not stay and fight. He thought he was reshaping humanity, paving the way for stronger, better creatures to inhabit the world. We were about to show him just how wrong he was.

I'd be lying if I said I wasn't nervous. We'd been on reconnaissance missions and had painstakingly gathered every little detail and every weapon we could get our hands on. We knew the inner workings of his demon court and the time the guards rotated posts when we could slip in unnoticed. Yet, I still felt underprepared. The feeling in my gut told me that there was something sinister, a weapon we'd never laid eyes on, one he'd kept a secret. It would be just like him, conniving and sneaky, to be able to ensure his rule. He'd made slaves out of those who had bowed down to him. They were treated like the dirt on the bottom of his boots, expected to please his crazy whims, and were given nothing in return.

They were way worse off than us. Yes, we lived in constant danger, having to switch hiding places every week lest he find out about us, but at least we had our own wills, the strength to do what needed to be done.

As I looked at all the faces surrounding me, pale, but shining with virtue, I hardened my resolve. Some of them were kids, barely adults. I'd found several of them squatting in dumpsters and hiding out in alleyways before I'd brought them here and trained them to fight, to be warriors. They'd lost their families to the attacks, eventually gaining new ones here. After all, the strongest bonds were formed during the most perilous times. I imagined ours like a rope weaved of light, anchoring us and keeping the darkness at bay. If not to what little was left of the world, we owed it to ourselves to fight, and to give them hell. So, with renewed courage and vigour, I declared, "March. To battle."

If we died, we died together.

With each step, we got closer to the centre of the city, closer to his palace. My boots crunched with gravel mixed in with the bones of the dead. Every time I stepped on anything that looked like a bone, my heart lurched, and bile rose in my throat. I didn't understand how he could do this. He was human after all, maybe twisted and warped, but still human. His pale face flashed across my mind. His cold sneer, the maniacal quality to it that labelled him demented. His cold grey eyes, constantly swirling like a volcano about to erupt. I had seen exactly what happened when he did erupt. That fateful day came back to me. The day I'd lost everything.

My father and I had just gone out to try and hunt for food, any scraps that we could find, when he'd shown up with his demon cronies. They'd cornered us in an alleyway, holding us at knifepoint. We'd been forced to walk to his palace, the only thing in this city that gleamed, its spires rising up into the sky. His growling demons had held my father captive, while one pulled out a metal whip. I could never forget the genuine terror in his eyes as he comprehended what they meant to do to him. I'd lurched forward, trying to save my father, offering myself up as a sacrifice instead, but he'd only laughed and commanded a demon to hold me back, who did so with a grunt.

I'd watched in horror as the demon brought the whip down on my father's back one, two, three times. I'd watched the gashes open up, blood welling and gushing down his bent body, his face beaded with sweat, contorted in pain. Tears slid down my face, my hands out in front of me, pleading, begging him to have mercy on us. And he'd just laughed a deranged laugh, the sound rising and echoing in the chamber. I watched my father die that day, my only living family. It was the day I'd sworn to myself I would destroy him. End him once and for all.

A flash of movement caught my eye and I jumped into my defensive stance immediately. From the corner of my eye, I saw my friends do the same. A tiny demon slithered into view. One swipe of my knife had me severing its head. I breathed a sigh of relief, too soon it seemed, because in that instant, an alarm started to blare all around us, and the commander of all these demons himself sauntered into view.

"Coming to try and kill me?" He asked with a smirk. "I'd like to see you try." He raised his arms upwards and all his demons assembled. There were so many everywhere, all of them surrounding us from all sides. I steeled myself. Glancing sideways, I saw a similar resolve in everyone's eyes and I smiled. His arms came forwards and the demons charged at once.

Everything became a blur. Hacking, slashing at demon limbs, their blood washing the streets red. I whirled about in a deadly arc, my knives flashing before me. I didn't know how long I did this for, until at once, all motion seemed to still. We'd killed them all, every last one. I saw his face go slack, astonishment in his eyes. Grinning, I raised my gaze to meet his. The fury in it didn't startle me, didn't throw me off. I was an angel, avenging my losses, a golden glow almost emanating off me. He gaped, stunned.

In his split second of confusion, I threw my knife with deadly precision and lethal accuracy. It flew straight and true, embedding itself into his heart. I saw the frenzy of emotions play out on his face. The bewilderment, which quickly turned into outrage, then in his last moment, finally the acceptance before he sunk to his knees and the light behind his eyes died.

As his hold over the world lifted, the sun rose once more, radiating with light. Its warmth soaked into my bones, a warmth I hadn't felt in years. I tilted my face up towards the ball of burning fire and closed my eyes, letting myself relax for the first time in five years. As I looked around at the faces of my fellow rebels, battle-scarred and bloodied, I felt a grin sneaking up on me, lifting the corners of my lips. They looked exhausted; I could see it in the bags under their eyes. Yet, they were smiling right back at me, content for the first time since I'd found them.

ABOUT THE AUTHOR

I'm a fifteen year old high school student and the author of *Turn On the Light*. I've been an avid reader ever since I can remember and am known to devour eight hundred page novels in a day. I distinctly remember the library in Bangkok that felt enormous to four year old me, where I spent hours and hours learning to read. I love to swim, especially after a hectic day at school (which, yes, I know will become more and more hectic through the next two and a half years of high school).

I'm an Indian expat who's lived in Dubai with her parents for about eight years now. We live in an apartment where I love curling up on the couch with a bowl of ice cream and watching Gilmore Girls.

www.ingramcontent.com/pod-product-compliance
Lightning Source LLC
LaVergne TN
LVHW061345080526
838199LV00094B/7377